Minecraft: Battle at Creeper Fields

A Minecraft Novel

by Mari Cinco
& Best Minecraft Novels

Chapter 1: A Need, But a Hazard

It was the middle of nowhere and yet it was a place that stuck to the minds of all in the great Grassland biome: Creeper Fields. For miles and miles, Grass tall and trimmed stretched out without any trace of trees, mountains or structures protruding from the ground whatsoever.

It took five days on horse just to reach the closest forest and city. It took even more on foot. At night, monster mobs spawned in thick clusters of Zombies, Skeletons, Endermen…and Creepers, of course. It was an area as hellish as the Nether itself. But Leon and his men were going through it no matter what.

The Diamond Village stood at the northern border of Creeper Fields behind a high wall of cobblestone lit with torches splitting the fine line of safety and danger. The head of the village, Lord Japheth, had requested Leon to reach the other side of Creeper Fields and send a message to their allies in Emerald City.

"I need you to deliver this message within ten days," Lord Japheth said with a strong sense of urgency in his voice. He handed over a parchment envelope sealed with wax. "The

Alliance depends on it and if it's not delivered in time, bad things are going to happen."

"My men and I will send the message as soon as we can," Leon said as he lowered himself into a bow. "We won't let anything stop us from doing so."

Lord Japheth nodded and, though pleased, a grim expression fell upon his face.

"I'm sure you realize that this isn't a simple task I'm asking of you," Lord Japheth said. "The only way to get to Emerald City is to pass by Creeper Fields. We cannot risk sending messages by hawk, owl or any winged creature. The danger of the Gold Legion getting its hands on it is far too great."

Creeper Fields. The name rung inside Leon's head like a large church bell. A part of him wanted to tear away refusing, but another part was more than happy to do it. In the large study room of Lord Japheth, Leon stood from his bow. He placed a hand over his chest in salute.

"You can count on us," Leon said.

"I know I can," Lord Japheth said. "Send with you your fifteen best men and I will provide steeds, mules, blocks, food and the finest armory. It is ten days walk by foot, but by horse you should get there in half the time at the very most.

Lord Japheth looked at Leon, almost apologetically.

"I do not want to risk the men of our village," Lord Japheth said. "But this message not being sent may risk not just our village, but the Alliance as well. Please understand."

Leon gave a reassuring nod.

"My men and I are honored to be given the task," he said. "Worry not."

He left the room and though it was supposed to have been a private thing, the word spread around the village like wildfire—which it might as well have been. The townsfolk were appalled. Terrified, perhaps. At the town square, since Leon knew the word was already around, he answered the questions, concerns and worries of the people. He also answered protests.

"You can't go out there!" a Baker exclaimed near the front seats. "You'll die out! The mobs will come in dozens!"

"We guards have been serving the Diamond Village for twenty years. I can assure you we are experienced enough to fight," Leon said. "If it eases you any further, we'll be making shelters at night."

"What about the Creepers?" the town Butcher said. "What if they destroy your resources!? If you're not killed, you'll starve to death!"

"We'll manage the resources we have," Leon answered. "It's not like it's the first time we went days on with only slices of bread to eat and a bucket of water to drink from."

"Is the message so important that we must lose a third of our only defense line!?" yet another villager cried.

"If Lord Japheth says it is, then it is," Leon replied.

The questions were more or less of that nature and it left Leon anxious by evening. It wasn't the reason he couldn't sleep, though. No, his reason ran deeper than that. In fact, Creeper Fields had laced his sleeps with nightmare for years now. But none of this mattered and the mission did in all its being.

By next morning, everything was ready and the selected men waited at the high stone gates. The sun had hardly risen and the Diamond Village glowed in a pink-orange twilight. The air was cold and Leon's usually pale face was red at the cheeks from the harsh wind. Like everyone else, he wore Iron armor with Chainmail underneath. His stature as captain did, however, let him wear a dark blue cloak with a Diamond clasp. He stood in front of his men on his white horse, pulling back the leads as he whinnied in excitement to run out into the biome. From behind him, he could hear some of the soldiers mutter.

I've fought mobs before, one soldier said. But to go into Creeper Fields is crazy!

I know how you feel, another said disdainfully. Remember Jacob the Miner?

The first one seemed to groan in imaginary pain.

That was a horrible sight...he said.

Leon knew Jacob the Miner and he definitely remembered what happened to him. Everyone in Diamond Village would and should have after that horrible accident.

***

Jacob the Miner earned his title after single-handedly mining twenty blocks of Diamond in a ravine near the desert. No one had dared join him because it was outside the wall. Also, Jacob was known for his crazy exploits.

"Why on earth should we only mine in the village?" he had said in the square. "We can't wait until all our resources finish before we travel knew places! By then, it'd be too late! How many blocks of Iron, Coal and Stone can one mine shaft provide!? If we don't move now, by the time we need to mine somewhere new, we won't even have resources for that!"

"That's enough!" Leon had cried from the crowd.

With three men, Leon tried to contain Jacob from thrashing back and forth. His hazel green eyes, a rare color in the diamond village where eyes were blue, glared at Leon as they gripped his arms.

"Let me go!" he cried. "You want this village to survive, don't you, Captain!? It's your job! Let me help by doing mine!"

Leon pushed aside the remark and tied Jacob's wrists in thick knots of rope.

"You're speaking nonsense," Leon said. "You're just a kid. You can't mine alone. Especially not in a desert!"

Jacob had to spend a night in the village prison. So he can clear his mind, Leon had convinced himself. But that night only made Jacob want to go even more. Jacob was only sixteen but he had figured out how to dig past the guards using the village's mine shaft and came back after a week missing. With sooty hands, ruddy cheeks and enthusiasm beneath fatigued eyes, Jacob brought Diamonds in abundance along with other resources. He had also built a Rail track so people could automatically mine there.

Later that day, Lord Japheth proclaimed him a hero and Leon was honored to place a finely made Gold medal embedded with Diamonds around Jacob's neck. Jacob looked up to the captain, but not in a gloating manner.

"I did it," Jacob said. "I just had to believe and I did it."

Leon couldn't help but smiling and nodding.

"You did, kiddo," he had said that day. He then tousled Jacob's blonde hair and left the stage, leaving the boy to the villagers' cheers.

And then the next week came. Jacob dropped by Leon's office in the Guard Tower. Leon didn't know how he had come to be a source of admiration to the boy, but Jacob went to him that day saying Leon would be the first to know about his great plan.

"I'm going to build a path through Creeper Fields!" Jacob burst in excitement.

Leon knocked his Ink jar with his elbow. Black liquid pooled onto the table like runny paint. Leon leapt from his seat and slammed his hands on the table.

"Are you nuts!?" Leon shouted.

He immediately regretted it when Jacob's face dropped in dejection. Leon relaxed his shoulders and shook his head.

"I'm sorry I yelled," Leon said. "It's just that…no one has ever ventured through Creeper Fields. It's a long stretch of land with no structures for miles. Mobs plop there like drops in a storm, I hear. You can't risk that, can you? Think about your mother."

Jacob's eyes raised themselves up to Leon's own azure ones apologetically.

"I'm sorry, Captain," Jacob said. "I didn't mean to surprise you like that." And then, with a little more conviction, "But I know what I'm doing."

"Do you?"

Jacob paced back and forth the office, looking at the ground, his mind hard at work as he explained everything. The sun was setting that moment and it made Jacob's hair faintly glow in the light. Jacob's mother had that same kind of hair. She was a beautiful woman and a simple baker. Most of all, she worried about Jacob. Leon couldn't imagine how she had felt when Jacob had left to mine in the desert.

"I want to shake fear out of the village..." the boy said. "Let them know there's something more than mobs waiting out there. And what about the Emerald City? We're long-time allies with them and only by what? Hawk mail?"

"The Alliance can coexist by such means," Leon said. "But going through Creeper Fields is absurd! What will you have for shelter if there isn't anything to build upon!?"

"I'll build shelter underground," Jacob said. "Or bring my own Cobblestone if I need to."

Jacob then placed both hands on Leon's shoulders, a dead seriousness in his eyes.

"I can do this," Jacob said. "But only if you let me!"

"Only if I let you?" Leon said. "You're forgetting Lord Japheth. You're mother. The entire village!"

"They trust you on this, Captain," Jacob argued. "Give your word and everyone will follow. They trust your good judgment!"

Leon's heart was pounding now and a fine, thick-beaded sweat line traced his brow. You can't make me responsible for this…Leon said. You just can't…

"I already have a team," Jacob added. "We have enough resources for a week and we can mine for the rest."

You can't make me responsible for this…please don't let me be the final word…

"Please, Captain?" Jacob asked. "Just trust me. Please."

Leon looked away from the boy. He started out the window where a wall blocked whatever sight there probably was of the outside. It was true. The village did live in fear of mobs. Leon and his men could handle the monsters that tried to breach borders, but what was beyond that? What had always been beyond that? Here was Jacob, a young boy so much braver than him that wanted to find out the answers.

Leon closed his eyes painfully.

"I'll let you do what you will," he said in a coarse voice. "But on one condition."

"What's that?"

It was Leon's turn to place his hands on Jacob's shoulders. It was his turn to stare directly into Jacob's eyes gravely.

"Come back…" Leon said. "Come back, Pickaxe and all."

Leon thought he had seen a tear leave Jacob's right eye. The boy nodded, his smile trying to fight back a cry of happiness.

"Yes, sir."

Leon watched Jacob go with five other miners and two guards (new recruits and good friends of Jacob). On a Horse, Jacob waved his miner's hat wildly at Leon, his face saying everything for him: I'm on my way. I promise to make you proud. From the gates, Leon watched Jacob disappear into the horizon with the square sun setting down on them, feeling more hope than fear in so long. It was as if he was as sure as the sun would rise again in the morning.

They didn't last a day.

By dusk on the day after, people gathered at the gates as they heard the shrill cries of someone asking for the gates to open.

"Let me in!" the wail begged. "By Mojang, don't let me stay outside another minute! DON'T!"

The guards were swift to rush to the gates and draw the bridge, but Leon was paralyzed. The light feeling in his chest was replaced with a heavy block of Iron. His hands began to tremble and a cold sweat was running on his back. He almost thought he'd stay that way forever. There was a stone in his throat, but instead of choking when he spoke, he yelled loudly.

"What the heck are you doing!?" he cried as he ran to through the crowd. "Give him space! Get an Aid NOW! Move! Move! MOVE!"

Oh, Mojang…he begged. Let it be him! Let it be him! PLEASE!

But it wasn't him. It was Tracy, Jacob's mining partner from the shaft. Seeing him instead of Jacob felt like Leon's mind dropping to his feet. Tracy was crying, his clothes now just scraps, his face ruddy not from mining, but from surface dirt, and his hands carrying something wrapped in cloth…Jacob's shawl. Practically sobbing himself to convulsion, Tracy stood in the middle clinging with dear life to the cloth-covered object. Leon knelt down before him the same way he would kneel down before Mojang's altar in fervent prayer.

"What happened?" Leon said in a whisper.

"It was horrible!" Tracy cried. "It was horrible! So many monsters! There was no underground! After one block, it's Bedrock!"

The village people gasped in horror.

Bedrock!? One cried.

That's impossible! A second said.

Insanity! A third yelled.

The village people mumbled and yelled and whimpered. The sound doubled in volume in

Leon's ears. Tracy sat there, crying as well. He rocked back and forth in a small block, shaking his head.

"SILENCE!" Leon cried. The village people went silent and stared at him. With glaring eyes, Leon continued. "Let the boy finish! And where is that aid!?"

The aid, a girl in a white long-sleeved dress came and tried to approach Tracy. She knelt down.

"We're gonna clean your wounds," the girl said in a trembling voice. She reached out to Tracy.

"DON'T TOUCH ME!" Tracy cried.

The girl was so taken aback, she fell backward, her eyes huge with shock. She looked at Leon but he raised a hand to calm her down and he drew closer to Tracy.

"Tracy," Leon said again. "You're badly hurt. Let us fix you. Where are the others?"

The last question was hard to say without trembling as well, but Leon said it and he waited for an answer. Tracy looked up at Leon, first in confusion then understanding. He then shook his face as it writhed again to form a sob. Tracy covered his eyes with his free arm. He continued to shake his head.

"Where are they, Tracy?" Leon repeated; his voice at the edge of losing control.

"No…" Tracy muttered. "Just…no…"

Leon grabbed Tracy firmly by the shoulders and shook him hard.

"Where are they!?" Leon yelled.

"THEY'RE GONE!" Tracy wailed.

Tracy's scream was loud enough to echo against the tall walls of the village and yet Leon couldn't hear what he had said. Tracy began crying again, his head stooping down almost as low as the ground, gasping in the middle of his cry to breathe.

"They're all gone!" Tracy said again. "The Creepers blew up our only shelter in seconds…the guards didn't last a minute! They're all gone!"

Leon slumped backward and stared at Tracy for a while, his energy had left him entirely. There was only one more question. One confirmatory question. One that could still be his hope.

"Jacob?" Leon whispered.

Tracy looked at Leon and then the clothed object. He raised it out in his arms, offering it to Leon.

"Jacob…" Tracy said. "He told me…to tell you…he can only make half his promise…"

Leon took it, in denial of what was probably inside the cloth. His hand hovered over the fold and then pulled it. From the distance, Jacob's mother screamed in agony and fell to the ground weeping. Leon probably didn't stare at the object for more than a minute but it was long enough to burn into his memory for the rest of his life. In the cloth was a rusting pickaxe, the name Jacob etched into a wooden handle.

***

"Captain?" a voice called. "Captain?"

Leon shook his head to regain his senses. He felt for sure he had been reliving the moment he found out Jacob was gone. But it was only a memory. Leon looked now as his second-in-command, Gabe, stared at him in concern from his brown, white-spotted steed.

"Captain Leon," Gabe said. "Are you alright?"

Leon looked at the ground and back at Gabe.

"I'm fine," Leon nodded.

"The gates open in a few minutes," Gabe said.

"Alright," Leon replied. "Just hold on for a minute."

Leon got off his horse. It was a thing he thought of at the last moment and he was quite surprised he had forgotten to do what he did every morning at dawn. He marched over to an elevated level of land where a few gravestones were. To the left side, touched by the sun, was Jacob's headstone. Leon took out a dandelion he had picked in a wild patch of grass.

"I'm going where you went," Leon said. "I think I understand now. I understand why you wanted to pass through Creeper Fields. It's a need. It's a need even if it's a hazard. And I will cross it the way you wanted to. I promise that…my son."

A small tear left his eye but no one would have known it. Leon marched back to his men and sat back on his horse.

"Alright, men!" Leon said. "Today we're going to pass through a place as dangerous as the Nether itself! We know it sounds impossible, but we need to fulfill the mission for our village and the Alliance. Today, we will make history as the first troop to have ever fully passed Creeper Fields!"

Chapter 2: The First Night

Fifteen men and a captain traveling throughout Creeper Fields with only horses and a few resources…it was a troubling thought. It was also admirable. The draw bridge opened slowly. Its chains clinked repetitively like the ticking of a clock as pulled back into the giant reels at the side. Little by little, the sun peered through the crack, first a slivery golden line, then a thick ray, and then…

"How beautiful," Gabe said under his breath.

Warm bright light poured over the soldiers as the sun lifted from the horizon and into the square sky. Grass blocks stretched out in a wide flat plain, tall grass scattered over it in disorganized clusters. The water below the draw bridge rushed and bubbled and it gave, too, a golden glow in the sunlight.

"Beauty can be death," Leon answered to Gabe's comment.

Gabe, with his sand colored hair and light blue eyes, looked at Leon in an agreeing manner. Leon's horse stepped out first and then he jerked his head out into the wilderness.

"Let's go, men," he said briskly.

The men followed with the mules carrying their supplies lingering behind and being tugged by leads. The twilight eventually gave way to a bright day and the men picked up their speed. The horses galloped through the scenery. There used to be rail tracks here…Leon thought. Yes, that was when Jacob came here. Grief stricken, Leon demanded the guards to tear them away so that no one would ever have to go through it again or even have the idea to cross Creeper Fields. It's ironic that I'm here even if it isn't funny, Leon thought.

***

The men were more than happy to sit down and eat. It was more of fighting off anxiety rather than being exhausted. Leon looked them all over by face. There was Gabe, of course, to his right. There was Mark, Nate, Joe and Steve…there was…

"Wait a minute," Leon said aloud.

He walked over to the corner where a young man in chain armor was sitting down and peeling a baked potato.

"Hey," Leon said sharply.

The boy looked up. He was just about to eat the potato, but dropped it upon hearing Leon's voice. The boy fumbled upwards, his chain mail uniform, obviously too big for him, dangled and swung to and fro. He was a blonde kid with electric blue eyes and a smile that probably meant mischief when he wanted it to be.

"S-sir!" the boy stammered. He finally managed to sit up straight and give Leon a salute.

Leon raised a brow.

"I don't remember you," he said. "What's your name?"

"Kai, s-sir."

"That's captain, to you."

"Yes, Captain!"

From behind him, Leon could hear the other guards snicker. He gave them a small glare to quiet them. He then turned back to see Kai smudging away bits of potato peel from his fingers.

"Now I remember," Leon said. "You're the new recruit aren't you?"

Kai smiled and nodded.

"Yes, sir! I, uh, mean, Captain!" Kai said excitedly. Leon frowned and Kai's face drooped. Leon loomed over him and sneered.

"What on earth are you doing here!?" he yelled. "I brought with me my best fifteen men! I don't need an inept little…"

He looked around and then he noticed…the men were only fifteen.

"Who's missing?" Leon demanded everyone. The men turned away or tried to occupy themselves with eating. Leon glared at Kai.

"I can answer that," Kai said nervously. "Sir Barra…he didn't want to go. I asked if I could trade places with him. He gave me ten iron ingots for letting me go in his stead…"

Leon's hand came to the wool collar of Kai's undershirt and lifted Kai high up.

"He what!?" Leon shouted. "This Isn't an exploit people can pay for! This is a mission! And you accepted that!?"

Kai's smile was now far gone and it was replaced with genuine worry. Dangling in the air, Kai lifted up his hands in surrender.

"I'm s-sorry, sir! I mean, Captain!" Kai said. "Please, don't be mad! I wanted to go on the mission! I thought it would be wrong if Sir Barra just left with no replacement."

"How things are handled are up to me," Leon snared. "And you can bet that after this mission, you and Sir Barra will be getting to know each other a lot more in the dungeon sleeping on Haystacks and eating rotten Apples!"

He then pushed Kai aside on the square wooden planks of Oak, making him tumble. Gabe approached Leon and softly said, "Captain, perhaps we should send the boy home. He won't make it out here."

Leon shook his head.

"It'll be dark before he gets back to Diamond Village," he said. He gave the boy a quick look over as Kai dusted his leggings and pulled away sticking tall grass.

"You can stay," Leon said gruffly. "But you're staying right under my nose because you can very well die out here."

Kai's worry melted away and his smile reemerged.

"Thank you, Captain!" he said. "I promise I won't be in your way anymore!"

"You're already in my way," Leon frowned.

Unable to understand at first, Kai realized Leon was trying to make his way to the Furnace they had set down. He flinched and then moved to the side. The other soldiers tried to suppress laughter. Gabe followed after Leon.

"I can't believe Barra would do something like that," Gabe said.

"Yeah," Leon said. "Barra's one of our bravest men. I won't blame him for not coming, though. He has five children. In fact, these men shouldn't be obligated to come on this mission if they found it so terrible. Their lives are at stake."

"They came all the same," Gabe said.

Leon nodded. The two sat down for their share of Pork Chops and though it was quite peaceful, the fact that there was nothing to protect them from the bright square sun's heat was irritating. Sweating in small white pixels, Leon stood up again to walk over to the Chests near the Fence made for the Horses and Mules.

As he drew nearer, something buzzed in his ear. It was a small sound and he imagined it was just his old age playing tricks on him. The sound grew louder and he now knew it wasn't a buzzing sound, but more of a hissing sound. Vibrating against ear canals and ear drums, it began vexing him until he realized it wasn't an imaginary sound at all. He turned to the corner of the fence and dug into one block of Dirt was square of red divided into round segments with a flickering string on top...TNT. Before Leon could even get close, the block blinked white and...

BOOM!

The sound of crackling, toppling blocks followed after and it was only then that Leon regained focus. As he shook away the ringing sound in his ears as an after effect of the explosion, the troops approached him and Gabe knelt down.

"Captain!" he exclaimed. "Are you alright?"

His body was aching, but the explosion had not come in contact with him. It had tossed him aside onto the ground, though, and his body was sore. There was the sound of clacking hooves.

"The Horses..." Leon muttered. And then, clutching Gabe's collar, "Fools! Get the Horses before they escape!"

Just as he had thought, the animals were getting away and so were the Mules carrying the supplies. Three men rushed after them and Leon stood up as fast as he could; his head still spinning. Some of the Horses had died and a single Saddle was left behind, floating on the Bedrock layer Tracy claimed lay under the single sheet of Dirt.

Leon shook the last bits of haziness out of him and rushed to see where the men were setting off to. The Horses weren't getting that far and the men were about to catch up with them. And then a speck of light green pixels came into view. Leon squinted and the green pixels began to create an outline of a thick stump with a square head on top of it. Black eyes and a black, jagged frown faced towards the Horses and the running men, somehow unable to see the threat ahead of them.

"Retreat!" Leon cried. "Forget the Horses!"

And just as the men heard, a Horse came into the Creeper's view.

Sssssssss.....!

There was a sharp and loud explosion and the men were thrown back. The strained neighs of the Horses and Mules filled the air only for a second and it was followed by silence. Leon and Gabe rushed towards the men, all three without injury. It was then that Gabe said something.

"The supplies…" Gabe's voice was strained.

Out in the distance where the Creeper had exploded, all that was left were a few pieces of food and a couple of block stacks. In the Chests, there was even less. Leon walked up to the site, his hands balled up into fists.

"Who..." he started. "Who did this...?"

And then, with anger rising in his voice.

"Who did this!?"

The soldiers looked at him, confused about what he was referring to and none answered. Gabe came to his side and whispered.

"All of the soldiers were far away from the setup," he said. "Do you think someone else was here?"

"I don't know," Leon said. "It could have been a sneaker from the Gold Legion. Or...it could be one of our own men...but I don't want to raise suspicions when we need trust here the most. Just don't let anyone out of your sight and don't let anyone wander anywhere alone."

Gabe went over to the left over Items scattered across the ground. Plop, plop, the sound went as the Items turned over to his Inventory. As Gabe went over it, he looked at Leon gravely.

"This will only last fifteen men, at the most, three days," Gabe said.

Leon covered his face with his hand and pressed on his temples. He then looked up.

"We'll have to tell the men, then," Leon said.

He looked to the sky. It was still scorching bright, but on foot, they weren't going to get far.

"We should set up for the night, too," Leon said. "I'm sure no one is gonna want to walk the day knowing we won't have that much food."

It wasn't the food that was worrying Leon, though. It was the TNT. Who could have set it there and why?

***

Dusk fell fast and with the stacks of Cobblestone they still had, they managed to create five small Cobblestone huts, each one occupying three soldiers. They had the beds ready, but everyone was nervous for the night.

"Don't bother with wooden Doors," Leon instructed his men. "If Zombies break it down in your sleep, you'll end up as one of them, too. Fit all huts with Iron ones. And remember, only half a slice of Bread tonight for everyone."

For a while, the rectangular sky was once again filled with the orange-pink tinge of twilight. The color quickly darkened into a dark blue dotted with small white pixels of stars. With Torches lighting a ten by ten radius outside the circle of huts, the men retired.

"We can't appreciate the stars this much in the Diamond Village," Richard, the oldest guard and one-eye blinded, remarked.

He was sitting on his Wool Bed facing Leon and Gabe.

"The Beacon disrupts the night sky, doesn't it?" Leon agreed. "But we can't manage without light at night. The mobs grow too thick. I can only bet that outside our light radius, Creepers are wondering about."

"What was that commotion earlier over the Horses?" Richard asked. "I heard the explosion twice. Were they wandering Creepers?"

Leon and Gabe gave each other a sideward look.

"I don't think so," Richard said. "That first explosion was far too wide to be only a Creeper. It had to be two…wait, no. I'd have heard three explosions then. It must have been TNT!"

Richard's filmy blind eye stared blankly at the two soldiers knowingly. Leon sighed.

"Yes," Leon said. "I actually saw it when it was set. It exploded before I could stop it."

Richard's face changed from knowing to confusion. He lifted his arms in question.

"Why on earth didn't you say anything in front of the troops?" Richard said. "We'd be far more on our guard! It must be those Dirt buckets from the Gold Legion!"

"Sir Richard," Leon said. "I have a feeling it's not someone outside our troop. Creeper Fields has no structures that allow sneaking or otherwise. We'd have seen an intruder immediately."

"Are you saying it's someone from inside the group?" Richard asked unsurely.

Leon gave a brief nod. Richard shook his head, not in disagreement, but in disbelief.

"If we have a traitor…" Richard said. "Everyone would become suspicious of everyone else…"

"That's right," Gabe agreed. "What we need is to make sure we can stick together as a team. If we break down apart…it would jeopardize the mission."

"I think our food supply alone would drive everyone insane," Richard said.

Leon winced at that remark. For the next days, they would have to travel by foot. There was no other option. Travelling on foot would mean at least a ten day's walk. There were no comments from the soldiers, but Leon knew a difficult road lay ahead for them.

Urrrgh…ruurrrh..

He could hear the sound of zombies from outside. Using the single Glass Pane window of the hut, Leon looked outside. Zombies were wandering around, but not yet within closer proximity to the light radius.

Leon was used to seeing this from the Guard Towers and the Wall Patrol in the village. He was even used to nightly combat with Zombies that came too close to the Village walls. However, the Zombies here came in much bigger groups and their behavior seemed…erratic—disorganized. Usually, Zombies headed straight for the Doors and started banging on them. These Zombies were doing the opposite. They were wandering outside the light as if the Iron doors didn't matter.

This is a good thing. Why should I be worrying? Leon thought to himself.

The next sound he heard was that of Endermen teleporting around. Pah! Pah! Pah ! The eerie sound they made when they puffed out of thin air or teleported out of their area.

Well, Endermen are harmless as long as we're in here, Leon reassured himself.

He then heard rattling. Klak, klak, klak! The sound of the Skeleton warriors' bones as they walked to and fro. They, too, were staying out of the light's radius.

Our Torches aren't the sun, Leon thought. Why are they staying away from it? Is there something I'm missing?

He drew closer to the window, trying to figure out what felt out of place with everything. For a moment, he saw the same thing he had seen earlier.

Something's just not ri—

SSSSSSSSSSSSSSSSSSSSSSssssssssssssssss sss….

BOOM! BOOM! BOOM!

Three explosions after the other flew into the night. The ground shook and Leon could hear the crumbling of Cobblestone.

"What was that!?" Gabe said.

"Creepers, you idiot!" Richard called from his side while unsheathing his Sword.

Leon drew out his own Diamond Sword and peered out the window as the mob charged down past the light radius and past their hut and to the one just ten blocks away from them. The hut's right wall had burst open and the three men there lay unconscious on the ground. The groans of Zombies, the rattling of the Skeletons, the roars of the Endermen were followed by the surprised shouts and agonized cries of Leon's men.

"Gabe, Richard!" Leon called. "We have to get out there!"

Leon was just about to pull the Iron Door's wooden Lever but Gabe stopped him short.

"Captain, you can't!" Gabe cried. "The mobs are too thick! We'll be killed! Let the other guards do it!"

"Are you nuts!?" Leon shouted. "I will not leave them out there! Stay if you will!"

Leon pulled the Lever and the door cranked open. Richard drew behind him and so did

Gabe, though in reluctance. As Leon looked no other huts had opened their doors.

Are they deaf to the sound or in deep sleep!? Leon thought. No. They were scared. Leon was about to rush past them but he was pushed aside by a stream of mobs. Surprised, he gripped his sword and Richard was about to jump in attack, but the mobs paid no attention to them. They were all heading to those damaged by the Creepers.

"Let's go!" Leon cried to his two companions. "That's Marcus, Cardin and James!"

"HELP!" the sounds came from the huts.

"We've been breached!" Another cried. "Everyone, we've been breached!"

"Hold on!" Leon yelled. He then charged forward, swinging his blade in furious frenzy, each Zombie taken down by a single hit. Gabe followed behind with a Bow, hitting the mobs farther away from him.

"ALERT!" Richard cried in his old voice as he banged on the other doors of the soldiers. "WAKE UP! WE'VE BEEN BREACHED!"

Forced out of their huts, the troops emerged, but Leon was already way ahead and scraping clean the path of mobs.

"Hold on!" Leon called. "Hold on!"

But the moment Leon got there, the men were no longer crying and as he soon saw, the men in their Iron Armor had been replaced by Zombies wearing their attire.

"No…" Leon said. "NO!"

He screamed in anger and rushed forward, Richard controlling the Zombies forming behind them.

Sssssss….

"Captain!" Gabe called.

A hand pulled back at Leon's cape and dragged him away from the hut as it exploded as second time. Cobblestone flew into the air.

"NOOOOOO!" Leon yelled.

"RETREAT!" Gabe called. "RETREAT BACK TO YOUR HUTS NOW! DOUBLE THE WALLS!"

Leon struggled wildly against Gabe's pulling, but it was coupled with Richard's thin, but strong arms now closing over him and yanking him back as well.

"We can't leave them!" Leon yelled. "We can't!"

"Captain, they're gone!" Richard said. "Get ahold of yourself! Don't risk yourself or any more men!"

But the mobs didn't seem interested in the troop anymore. After the second explosion of the

Creeper, they stopped barricading the destroyed hut and began walking…away. Slowly they left the light radius, the three new ones in their Iron Armor and Chain mail following them. Leon was pulled inside and the Iron Door shut closed. He pulled away from Richard's grasp and looked at the old man and Gabe with insanity in his eyes.

"Why…!" he started. "Why did you—"

But he stopped himself short and fell down to his knees shaking his head, silent.

"They were turned into mobs by the time we got there," Gabe told Leon. "It would have been futile to go after them. I'm…I'm sorry."

Leon shook his head.

"It's not your fault," Leon said coarsely.

He stood up again, exhausted from the short berserk state he had been in and limped toward his bed.

"Our Horses are gone and so are our supplies," Leon said. "And now our men. All within one night…"

Richard and Gabe looked to the floor. Richard shook his head of gray hair, again in disbelief.

"What menace runs this land?" the old man said to no one in particular. "What menace runs amok here in Creeper Fields?"

Chapter 3: Mounting Burdens

The first assumption Leon had made was that one of the men had left the hut and met eyes with a Creeper. Creepers didn't explode unless they came in contact with humans. Leon then announced that no one was to leave their huts unless called to do so.

"The mobs only attacked the hut blown up by the Creepers," Gabe said that evening. "When we went out to help, they didn't even look at us. Why do you think that is?"

"Creeper Fields isn't an ordinary place," Richard told them. "I doubt the mobs act like the ones at home. If they're targeting only those hit by Creepers, we really should stay clear of them. We shouldn't even look at them."

"Then we will have no windows," Leon said.

He told the soldiers to do the same and the windows were replaced with Cobblestone blocks. No one could sleep that night and Leon spent his time sitting on an Oak slab and peering through the Iron Door's hole from time to time. He saw the same thing happen. Zombies and other mobs spawning, but staying outside the light radius.

They're not acting random, Leon now realized. They're waiting. Just like they did last night. But no Creepers are going to explode without us outside.

As if on cue, three Creepers came into sight. Leon hid himself behind the door as Gabe and Richard watched. From the edge of his vision, Leon could see the Creepers moving towards another hut.

They're probably waiting for someone to come out, Leon said. Not tonight.

But the Creepers didn't wait. Instead they hurried towards the Iron Door of the targeted hut and began ramming it.

"Wait, what?" Leon said.

One after the other took turns ramming the door, each one going Ssst! as they did.

"They're damaging themselves!" Leon exclaimed in shock.

"What?" Gabe asked.

But Leon didn't answer. Fearfully, Leon watched from the Iron Door's peep hole. He watched as they did it again and then…they began flickering.

Ssssssstt….

Leon's blood ran cold and he yanked the door wide open.

"Christopher! Thomas! Kaleb! MOVE BACK!" he screamed to the soldiers of that hut.

BOOM! BOOM! BOOM!

The explosion was bright and Leon covered his eyes as he heard the Cobblestone hut burst open.

Uuuuuuurgggghh!

The cries of Zombies flooded the air and they rushed past Leon. Skeletons followed as well, shooting arrows towards the hut's direction. Leon stood still for a moment. Unable to believe it.

They directly attacked the hut…Leon thought. How…how is that…why…

"Captain!" Gabe called as he and Richard rushed to his side.

The events seemed to repeat themselves. The mobs surrounded the victims who were unconscious. Leon and the men fought off the thick mobs but were too late. By the time they reached the hut it was empty and new armored Zombies had joined the mobs.

"Captain, three Creepers to the right!" Richard shouted.

"Retreat!" Leon shouted. "And triple your walls! Don't let the explosions touch you!"

But just a few moments later it was sunrise and even the Creepers left the huts alone. Leon and the other soldiers surrounded the exploded site, all now suppressed level of Bedrock.

"Another three men!" Gabe exclaimed.

"And nothing to trigger the Creepers," Leon told them. "They're aggressive from the beginning. It doesn't matter if we don't bother them! They're after us!"

"What do we do?" a soldier named Lee said. "At this rate, we'll all be dead in three more nights!"

"This mission is hopeless!" another said.

"Enough!" Leon yelled. "We will not fail this mission! Lord Japheth said so himself. This mission could risk even our entire village! We'll find a way out of this!"

Even if the men were silent, Leon knew they were not reassured by his words. Not even Leon could believe his own words. Looking away, he faced to the direction they would be traveling.

"Let's get walking. And tonight, may no one sleep in a separate hut. We'll build a huge one with walls thick enough to withstand the Creepers from breaking it."

***

Orders went as followed and the men again walked with heavy hearts that day. The supposedly gentle sun now burned as hot as it would in the Desert. The underclothes and Chainmail seemed to stick to Leon's sweat ridden skin and his cape felt like a weight upon him.

Six men gone and only nine more, Leon said. Will anyone be left to read the message in Emerald City?

Thinking of the letter, he slipped his hand into a satchel at his waist and took out the envelope sealed with wax. A Diamond icon sat in the middle of the pressed blue wax, signifying it had come from the officials of the Diamond Village.

What message could it possibly be? Leon thought. I didn't bother asking before, but what could be so important that the lives of men are risked to deliver it by foot?

For a moment, he thought about opening it, but he decided against it. He didn't know who could be nearby trying to look at it. If the TNT did come from the group, they're bound to be after this.

Just as he tucked it back in, Kai walked to his side. Leon hadn't thought much of him the past days but he could see a significant change in Kai's disposition. He didn't carry himself laxly anymore. He walked fast and stiffly, his eyes staring blankly at the ground and his former smile now a grim straight line.

"You alright?" Leon said in spite of himself.

He still didn't like the kid, but he felt sorry that a new recruit had to see so many men die in less than a week. Kai lifted his face and tried to smile but failed.

"It's been a rough three days," Kai said.

"Yeah," Leon said. "Things are even more difficult than I could have imagined."

Kai nodded. They had walked a good few miles and the sound of the Grass brushing against their legs was a pain in Leon's ears.

"I always wanted to be a guard as a kid," Kai said out of the blue. "When I was young, I thought it was awesome to be a guard. Guards had cool weapons, flashy armor and were always in action. My father said I didn't have the guts to be a soldier. I passed the marks in combat classes…but just barely."

Leon could have vouched for that. Kai looked nowhere near physically fit. He was tall, yes, but hardly any muscle seemed to lie under his flesh.

"Why did you decide to come on the mission?" Leon said. "I'm sure there was more to it than just being given Iron Ingots."

Kai's face lit up a bit and for once it wasn't an irritating sight.

"I wanted to prove my father wrong, of course," he said. "I wanted to show him I could make him proud."

"Ah..." Leon said, vaguely remembering Jacob.

He didn't have long to reminiscence, though. Kai's face turned all dejected again and added:

"I didn't expect this to happen."

Leon shook his head.

"I told you, kid," Leon said. "This mission isn't a joke. Neither is being a guard. You're risking your life for others. It's not all about glory."

Kai gave him a brief nod.

"You're right," Kai said. "I'll try to remember that."

Kai then picked up his pace and walked past him.

***

The group was fortunate to have enough Cobblestone to build a three-roomed hut. The soldiers beds filled up the entire spaces and everyone retreated for the night, their exhaustion now beating away the anxiety that had kept them up the nights before.

"I'll keep watch by the door," Richard said. "You're eyes are getting heavy, Captain."

"I guess so," Leon admitted as he rubbed his temples. "But if you see a Creeper get in within even ten blocks, tell me."

Richard nodded, his smile ageless and wise.

"I'll take the first two hours and then we'll shift," Richard said. "I may look old but I can stay up longer than any of you."

Leon joined Gabe and lied down on the Bed next to his. No one bothered removing their armor. The fear of Creepers exploding the hut was far too great, they realized. Leon let the heaviness of sleep take over him and he realized Richard had lied to him because sunlight was pouring out the door when he opened his eyes again.

"Captain?" Gabe asked as his face loomed over his.

"What time is it?" Leon said as he sat up. He looked at his Clock and saw that it was around carly morning. Richard came in afterwards, a mischievous smile on his face.

"Why didn't you wake me?" Leon demanded.

Richard shrugged.

"You looked so peaceful in your sleep," Richard admitted. "I didn't have the heart to wake you or Sir Gabe. But anyways, we made it through the night!"

"Really!?" Gabe said in shock. "No Creeper break-ins, nothing?"

Richard shook his head.

"The Creepers acted strange last night," Richard said. "They just...stood outside the door, waiting."

"They didn't ram themselves in like before?" Leon asked.

"No. In fact, it was as if they knew they wouldn't be able to break the huts thick walls. It's all very disturbing, really."

Leon nodded in acknowledgement.

"It's as if the Creepers here were intelligent..." Leon's voice trailed off. "But anyhow, that means this setup will be effective for the next night as well."

"Hopefully," Gabe said. "Now, Captain, we should gather the rest of the men to bring it down and continue the journey."

Being in a better mood than ever before on the trip, Leon agreed and the three moved to the main room where a few other men were waiting. Upon seeing Leon, the other men began to cheer.

"We made it last night, Captain!" one soldier said. "You're plan was brilliant!"

"This should make things easier for the next nights!" Another soldier said.

"We'll make it through Creeper Fields for sure!" Yet another said.

"Last night was a triumph for all of us," Leon assured. "But remember, we have many nights to walk and we can only hope the best. We must never falter, though. We have to cross through Creeper Fields for the mission."

"The mission!" the men cried.

There was a loud roar of excitement and Leon pulled the lever of the door.

"Is everyone here?" he asked.

He looked around. There were only six men.

"Where are other the three?" he asked.

"Still asleep, probably," Gabe answered.

A shrill cry came from the last room in the hut. It filled the room, resonating against the Cobblestone walls and piercing the ears. It was a cry of terror and…agony. It was a scream that sent chills up everyone's spine. Leon looked to where the scream was coming from: the last room in the thick-walled hut. The wooden Door burst open, Kai coming out panting as two armored Zombies followed after him…Zombies that used to be men.

"HELP!" Kai cried. "HELP! They've turned into Zombies!"

For a second, Leon's blood ran cold…and then it began to boil. Kai rushed forward only to slip on the planks and the Zombie opened its mouth wide to attack him. Leon screamed and pulled out his Sword, rushing to Kai's aid. He swung, beheading the two Zombies in one swipe in front of the men frozen in shock. The Zombies' armor dropped to the floor and only the thing left of the Zombies were their heads.

The moment had blurred in front of Leon and now he found himself breathing heavily as Kai began sobbing in the middle of the room. Dizzily, he turned his head to Kai to ask what had happened, but no words came out.

"They turned into Zombies!" Kai wept. "We just woke this morning and they suddenly flickered and turned into Zombies!"

"That's not possible!" Gabe said. "We're inside! There are no Zombies here! How did that happen!?"

"I DON'T KNOW!" Kai yelled almost as loudly as Tracy did the day Jacob died. "I don't know!"

"Captain," Gabe said, in sort of question to Leon on what they should do next.

A stone formed in Leon's throat and he was still staring at the two Zombie Heads floating on the floor, waiting to be picked up.

"We have to leave," Leon said. "Everything. Don't bother with the hut. We have to go now. Who knows what will happen next."

"But the Cobblestone—" Gabe said.

"We have enough!" Leon said. "We have enough for another hut. Let's just…let's just leave…"

But despite Leon's words, the men stood still, paralyzed, save for Kai who was wiping his tears.

"LEAVE NOW!" Leon shouted.

The men huddled into single file and Leon held out his hand to Kai.

"Let's leave, kid," Leon said.

Kai shook his head wildly, pointing to the armor of his roommates.

"What about them?" he asked in a strained voice.

Leon didn't answer for a while. For a second, he could see the Zombie Heads, but he could also see the faces of Harry and Skye. Richard came from behind and placed a hand on Leon's shoulder.

"You didn't kill your men," Richard said. "Those were Zombies, Captain. Your men were already gone the moment they transformed."

Leon bobbed his head briskly.

"I know," he said, though unsure.

He swung an arm under Kai's body and helped him up with Richard supporting the boy on the other side.

There's no end to it…Leon thought. There's just no end to any of it here in Creeper Fields.

Chapter 4: A Foundation of Hope

Leon didn't understand. He didn't understand any of it. How was any of this happening? Why were Creepers intelligent and aggressive? Why were mobs only attacking those Creepers exploded? How did his two men, in the sanctuary of the hut, turn into Zombies when they hadn't been in contact with mobs in the first place?

Leon's men were walking ahead of him and when they did, he took out his Diamond Sword and began stabbing the ground.

Why? he said in his head. Why!? WHY!?

He dug and dug at it until the Dirt block came off. The Dirt block plopped into his Inventory, but Leon noticed that it wasn't Bedrock that was there, but a Chest.

"What?"

"Captain!" Richard called.

As Leon looked, Richard was heading back towards him. Leon noticed that Richard walked with a limp, but still effectively fast.

"Is something the matter, Captain?" Richard called.

"I've found something!" Leon returned. "It's a Chest!"

Richard hurried over to him where Leon was now kneeling.

"A Chest!?" Richard said. "What would a Chest be doing all the way here?"

Leon shook his head.

"I don't know," he said plainly.

"Well open it," Richard said.

"It could be a trap," Leon's eyebrows furrowed. "Let's take a few steps back first."

The two went five blocks backward and Leon drew his Sword. He used the tip to flip the Chest open. There was no explosion.

"It's a Written Book," Richard said.

Leon drew closer to the Chest and picked it up. Scratched out letters on the leather cover.

"The Fortress," Leon read.

"The what?"

"It reads 'The Fortress'," Leon said.

"No!" Richard cried in disbelief. He yanked the Book out of Leon's hand and began flipping through cracked pages as the two began walking again.

"What is it?" Leon asked.

"I only thought it was legend..." Richard said.

"A legend?"

Richard looked at him in excitement.

"Yes," he said. "When I was young and the wall was only half-built, there was talk about a fortress in Creeper Fields. Fifty blocks high and fifty blocks wide, Stone on the outside and unbreakable Obsidian at its core...It was supposed to be the sanctuary for those who travelled Creeper Fields. I always thought it was a myth!"

"And isn't it?" Leon asked.

"A book of old make legends told be true...they said," Richard answered as he continued to flip the blank pages. He stopped and pressed a finger to the middle of the book. "And this is it!"

Leon peered at the page to see a finely sketched castle on a plain flat land. Creepers far and wide scattered around it, but in the picture, no damage could be seen. Immobile Fortress was written above it with a flourish. Below the castle's picture were smaller words: I seek to slay the fields.

"Immobile Fortress," Leon said. "Are you saying this place you're talking about...this sanctuary...is real?"

Richard turned his gaze to Leon and looked at him solemnly.

"Yes," Richard said. "I think it is. And I think we're close by."

Leon could hardly believe it. Was it really possible? Could it be that a good thing such as a sanctuary fortress could lie in the realms of a place as devious and hazardous as Creeper Fields?

"Which way is it?" Leon said.

"It lies at the middle of the path from the sea to the earth," Richard quoted. "My parents told me it meant blue and green. In short, in between the Diamond Village and the Emerald City. We're bound to see it on our way!"

"That's...that's..." Leon didn't have the word for it. He was too shocked. He didn't know if he was supposed to feel elated or doubtful. His mind ached for something positive to enter it, but the chewing paranoia and the experiences of the past dreadful nights haunted him.

Richard grasped Leon's arm.

"It's hope," Richard said. "We have to tell the men about this!"

"But what if it's a lie?" Leon said firmly. "What if I get their hopes up and it's just a goose chase? What will happen then?"

But Richard only smiled.

"It's not a lie," Richard said. "I know you won't believe. Therefore, let's keep it to ourselves until we see it."

"If we see it," Leon said.

Richard, old but as excited as a little boy, shrugged.

"Alright," he said. "If we see it."

Leon nodded. Richard then grinned and pointed at Leon's face.

"Is that a smile on your face, Captain?" he asked teasingly.

Leon realized he was smiling. He nodded.

"It's nice to think of hope," Leon admitted to him. They continued to walk until Gabe came running toward them.

"Captain!" he called. "Are you alright? You're far behind? Do you need a break?"

Leon shook his head and then cupped his hands around his mouth.

"We're fine!" Leon said. "But let's have a break all the same."

* * *

The food had lasted this long only due to the fact that the men had dwindled down in numbers. However, there were only fifteen pieces of meat left and five pieces of Bread.

"This can hardly sustain us!" one of the soldiers revolted. "What are we gonna do when we run out!?"

"There's no animal mobs for miles!" the other cried.

"A week without food!" said another. "We'll starve to death if the Creepers don't kill us!"

"Shut your mouth!" a fourth said. "Just because you're hungry doesn't mean you'll get more!"

"I'm only saying the truth!"

"You're a bloody complainer!"

The two got into a fight and the others began joining in, shouting and arguing as they surrounded the Chest that contained the last pieces of food. Kai stood back in the crowd and saw Leon, Gabe and Richard coming his way.

"Captain!" Kai called.

Upon seeing the commotion, Leon ran towards him.

"What's going on?" he asked.

"The food," Kai said. "They're arguing over our last food supply!"

Leon looked over as two of the men began brawling in the middle, punching and pulling at each other. The other men raised their weapons cheering or booing. He moved closer with his Sword wielded.

"Enough!" he shouted.

He swung his Sword down onto the Chest's wooden top, making the two brawlers recoil in shock.

"How dare you!?" Leon shouted as he looked at all the men. "How dare you fight your own comrades when this entire land is against us!? We're supposed to be a team!"

The two men put down their weapons and looked down to the ground. They backed away as Leon propped his foot on the Chest wear his Sword's tip dug into.

"This mission of ours will probably be our hardest!" Leon told the troop. "Never have we lost so much men. Never have we had to tread the land for so long without rest. Never have we experienced the tragedy of suffering and, now, the possibility of starvation.

"You are all the best of the best the Diamond Village has to offer," Leon said. "You are all here because for years we have dedicated ourselves to serve the village and the Alliance. To protect it…at the risk of our own lives! For years we have believed that the good of our home is that before ours. We have defended the walls and the gates of our village believing in that ideal! Why should it change now!? Should ideals change just because we don't feel up to it!? No!

"We're Guards! We're the defenders of our village and the Grasslands! We're not going to give up now! We will never give up! Even if the last of us dies at the hands of a mob. Even if we perish from lack of water or food. We'll suffer to the end for our people! Because we. Are. Guards!"

"GUARDS!" the men cried out. They cried out in cheers, their roars now mighty and the fear seemingly had melted away. Leon then stood up on top of a Cobblestone platform.

"I have an announcement to make," Leon said as he gave a glance to Richard.

The men hushed down at once, ready to listen with new hearts ready to follow orders. Leon couldn't help but feel glad as he looked upon that sight and he was beginning to feel a little lighter, himself.

"Richard and I have found something that might lead us to a shelter," Leon said. "According to old legends, there is a fortress in the middle of the path going to Emerald City."

He raised up the Written Book and eyes fell upon it as if he were holding a bright Diamond to the sun.

"Our trusted friend, Richard, says it will not only provide us safety for a night," Leon said. "But also replenish our needs and supplies. If we find it, we can carry on with the mission with more food, weapons and material for shelter."

The men cried out in merriment, raising their stump arms in joy and jumping. But Leon lifted a hand.

"I cannot guarantee we will find this," Leon said. "But the fact is that there is a hope for us! Keep careful watch for it, or anything that may lead to it. If the Mojang spirits will it, then the Immobile Fortress shall be ours!"

The men cheered again, a sound which ordinarily would have been unorganized was music to Leon's ears. And as the cheers begin to hush, Gabe lifted out his own Iron Sword.

"To our Captain!" he yelled.

"The Captain!" the men cried.

"The Guards!" Gabe said next.

"The Guards!"

"And to the Alliance!"

"Long live the Alliance!"

Richard had been right. The Immobile Fortress could be the hope they needed. The cheers were so loud and so great, that no one recognized the one soldier sitting quietly in the center, shaded by the others' jumps and movement, smiling sinisterly and knowing he would soon crush all this hope of theirs.

***

"Daddy!"

"Yes, son?"

"I want to be a guard when I grow up!"

The father couldn't help but smile as his little boy
said those words. He was only six but the young
lad had taken his father's sword sheath and
cape, dragging them as he wore it with pride.

"I'll fight the mobs like you do, Daddy!"

"Are you sure you don't want to be something
else? It's a pretty dangerous job."

The boy paused for a little bit.

"I'm not scared."

"Of course you're not, my little boy. But I'm
already a guard. Don't you want to be something
else?"

The father had taken the boy into his lap and
they were now watching the Oak wood burn
softly in the fireplace. The boy looked up to his
father with bright eyes.

"A miner, then!" the boy said.

"A miner?"

The boy bobbed his head.

"Uh-huh. You also have to be bwave (he couldn't pronounce the 'r' sound all that well yet in all words)."

"That's nice. That's a good job you have there."

The boy giggled and jumped in his father's lap, pressing his weight slightly against his belly and making him give out a small gag but laugh all the same.

"I'll bring you Dye-ah-munds," the boy said. "I'll make you the best Sword ev-ah."

"I can't wait for that. I'll use it every time."

"I'll also make the biggest fo-trah...fo-treh..."

"Fortress?"

"Yes! The biggest Foe-twess ever! And you can guard it!"

"I'm sure you will."

The father and son then shared an embrace; the son's small arms barely reaching his father's shoulders while the father's arms covered the little boy completely.

"I love you, Daddy."

"I love you, too, Jacob."

"Captain?" Gabe called.

"Yes?" Leon asked.

"We've found it."

It was getting dark now, but Leon didn't feel as worried anymore. He went up to where Gabe was and then he saw what Gabe was seeing.

A tall stone castle stood just twenty blocks from them. There was a large draw bridge and surrounding the structure was a moat of lava. There were tall towers and flags and a balcony where a stained glass window showed a Diamond Sword with an Emerald stone in it. Leon's breath was taken away as his eyes looked it up and down: the most beautiful fortress he had ever seen. He almost didn't notice Richard at his side.

"We're here," he said. "At our foundation of hope."

Leon nodded, so moved his voice came out only in a faint whisper.

"Let us guard it tonight with all our might."

Chapter 5: Battle at Creeper Fields

Leon and his men stood in front of the large wooden drawbridge with hearts pounding in apprehension and excitement. A sign at the edge near the moat of lava read: What doth thou seek at the fortress divine?

"But how do we open it, Captain?" Gabe asked.

Leon took out the Written Book from his cape. He flipped through it gingerly until he came to the pages with the sketch of the Immobile Fortress. The sketch was beautiful and a spitting image of the fortress itself. But at the same time, it could not bring the same amount of joy as it did. His finger traced the paper until it landed on the words he had read earlier with Richard. He also noticed nearby it was the image of the man near the drawbridge, raising a right hand towards it.

Leon made a few estimations and stood near the drawbridge where the man approximately did. He also raised out his hand. In his mind he could hear a soothing, sharp voice, the sound of a violin. It asked him: What doth thou seek at the fortress divine?

"I seek," Leon said in a loud, firm voice. "I seek to slay the fields!"

From above the thunder clashed. Leon and the men looked up as the dark sky filled with brightness and a rod of lightning bolted down to the drawbridge's center. There was the sound of a clank. It was then followed by a long creeeeeeeecceeeeak sound and slowly the drawbridge lowered, its chains clanking and clinking as it did.

"It worked!" Gabe said. "I can't believe it worked!"

The drawbridge slammed down in front of them and then it began to rain. The small droplets shot out from the sky like water daggers, swift and sharp on the skin. Leon took out his Sword and pointed towards the inside.

"Onwards!" Leon cried.

The men roared in agreement and they marched across the drawbridge and the golden lava flowing at each side.

Uuuurrrgh…raaarrggggh…uurrrrggh…

Leon turned behind to see Zombies in the far distance, dark specks of green distorted by the rain's now heavy shower.

"Hurry!" Leon said. "Everyone inside!"

The men followed and ran behind him, their feet thumping on the thick Spruce Wood of the bridge. Once everyone was at the opposite side, Leon pointed to the two pulley contraptions that laid at each side of the bridge.

"Hoist them up!" he called.

Two men obeyed and began pulling it up. For a minute, Leon's heart pounded. They needed to get the drawbridge up in time. Slowly it lifted up as the Zombies and the other mobs drew closer and closer, but alas it shut and they were now within the safety of the Immobile Fortress.

"Half of the men find the food supplies," Leon called out. "And half search for materials. In an hour we meet back here before we retreat for the night!"

The men shouted a "Yes, Captain!" and split up. Richard and Gabe were left with Leon.

"I want to look around for a Map and other things, if that's alright," Richard said.

"Very well," Leon replied. "I'd like to know how far we are exactly from the Emerald City. There's bound to be a library here somewhere."

***

The library hadn't been hard to find. Upon walking straight through the Stone Brick corridors, the three had found a central stairwell leading to large Spruce Doors. The library was considerably big but a table stood in the center and the Map was lying there, as if expectant of Captain Leon and his men.

"We're about halfway there," Leon remarked as he measured the distances on the map.

"I got a report by a passing guard earlier," Gabe said. "There are Horses here. We can get there in half the time. Two to three days at the very most."

"That'll do," Leon said. "We'll get our supplies for tonight and then leave in the morning for an early start."

"It's like a dream to be here," Richard said out of the blue. "It was always my favorite tale as a kid and now, in my old age, I am here and at the best time, too!"

Leon smiled and agreed. He rolled up the Map and just as they were about to leave, Gabe called them from the corner.

"Captain," he said as he pointed to the inside of a Chest. "I've found some armor here."

Leon and Richard approached him as Gabe pulled out a Diamond Chest Plate and Leggings.

"You should wear these, Captain," Gabe said. "You go out in combat the most. And I really think you deserve it."

"I couldn't possibly," Leon said, but Richard gave him a nudge.

"No one else should be as deserving as you are," Richard said. "You are the Knight representing our humble village so you should wear the proper attire. Plus, it will go with your blue cape."

So Leon equipped it and he was actually pretty pleased with how it looked and felt. It was light, that was for sure, and moving around in it made him feel like he wasn't wearing armor at all. There had been new sets of Iron Armor, too, and Gabe collected these for the soldiers whose armor was wearing out.

Everyone met back at the main hall with good news.

"There's a bunch of livestock in the East Wing," one of the soldiers said. "We didn't kill them all, of course. We only took what we needed and we feed Wheat to them to replenish. We should have enough meat for five days."

"We won't need to travel five days," another said. "We found ten Horses waiting in the West basement. Pure colored, too, so I can tell they're much faster."

"That's good news, all in all," Leon said. "The chambers are on the second floor. I say we retire for the night and then wake early to ride."

The men agreed and made their way up where rows of red Wool beds waited for them under a chandelier.

"Now I can sleep like this!" Gabe said as he tested out one of the beds.

Leon let out a laugh as Gabe hopped around like a boy in the Bed, trying to get cozy.

"How old are you, Gabe?" he asked.

Gabe shrugged.

"I feel ten years younger," he said.

Leon shook his head and began to walk up to the Door leading to the balcony, wandering if the storm had stopped as it would make mobs spawn in the morning if it didn't. The Door itself was stained glass tinged in aquamarine colors. As Leon drew closer, he could hear the pattering of rain on the Stone floor outside.

I guess it hasn't stopped yet, Leon said as he turned around. And that's when he heard it.

Screeech…screech…

It was a brisk, gurgling screech that Leon could only recognize as one thing. He peered at the stained glass window, still hearing it. Screech! Screech! As he drew closer, he pressed his face to it, trying to see clearly.

SCREECH!

Big red eyes and a hairy black face flashed in front of him. A Spider! Leon opened the door and stabbed his Sword into it, making it whimper and fade into dust. What's a Spider doing here? He thought. He then recalled that no Spiders had shown up throughout the entire journey.

The ground began to shake, but it wasn't trembling. Thump. Thump! THUMP! The sound went as the room began to shake. The soldiers drew their Swords and Bows, wandering where it was coming from.

"What is that?" Gabe said as he joined Leon's side again. They were both on the balcony now and by the time Leon saw what was below, he turned pale.

Millions of Spiders waited at the edge of the drawbridge, hopping eagerly to get inside. Skeletons and Creepers lined up behind them as if they were an army of their own. The thumping continued and far off in the distance were dozens of Zombies in armor with a huge Mutant Zombie towering at fifteen blocks and wide as ten stomped its way towards the castle.

"We're under attack!" Gabe said in realization. And then, rushing to the room. "We're under attack! Soldiers, arm yourselves!"

Leon followed inside with his Sword held tightly in his hand.

"Guards!" he called out. "An army of mobs lies just outside theses gates with a monster like we've never seen before as their ally. Equip yourselves to the teeth and stay at all perimeters!"

Just as he said so, the castle shook and as Leon looked outside, the giant Mutant Zombie was carrying a large square boulder. Leon's blood ran cold and so did the men's as the Mutant hauled the boulder towards the drawbridge. A huge crash followed and the castle's drawbridge fell down in half, making a path for the mobs now pouring in.

"To your stations!" Leon called. "Don't give up for nothing! Tonight, we battle here at Creeper Fields!"

***

Half of the men rushed down to near the drawbridge to rebuild new walls. They hurried block after block to prevent them from passing in. Spiders leapt through them as they attacked from behind, only to have Leon slice them.

"Archers!" Leon called to those above on the walls. "Hit as many Creepers and Spiders as you can!"

The archers shouted in understanding and each took out arrows in fours and fives, setting them on fire with Torches and shoving them down.

. Leon began helping with rebuilding the wall as Gabe rushed back and forth with supplies for the Archers.

"I've got lava!" Richard called out. "I've got lava! Stand back all of you!"

The old man ran up the stairs with his two scorching buckets.

"Is the wall clear!?" Richard called from above.

One man put the last block.

"Single layer is complete!" the soldier cried out.

"POUR IT DOWN!" Leon cried. "Men, don't stop building the walls, they can still get in! Onto the second layer!"

From above, Richard set down the lava, now cascading and splitting like a firework into multiple showers. The mobs screeched and rattled and cried as the hot substance singed and melted them away.

"Where's the Mutant!?" Leon said.

"Ten blocks away from the bridge!" Gabe announced. "He's coming with another boulder."

"Shoot him down!" Leon called. "Shoot him down and stop at nothing!"

From above, Gabe saw the Mutant slug itself towards the drawbridge and trying to tear down the wall. It's hand caught onto the lava and it roared loudly, taking a step back and squashing the second line of Zombies.

"Their dwindling down!" Gabe said. "The mobs are dwindling down!"

Leon rushed up to where Gabe was, sweating and adrenaline pumping through his veins. The lava hissed and hissed, burning down the mobs like a grinding outer wall. One by one they began to fall and disappear.

"We still have to deal with the Mutant," Leon said. "He's not taking damage to the Arrows. He'll need melee damage."

"That's insane!" Richard said. "How on earth can we take him out with those mobs running out there!?"

As Leon looked down at the Mutant, the monster bent down to see to its burning hands. Its nape bare and only veins popping out of it like rectangular snakes. Leon turned to Richard and Gabe.

"You don't need to," Leon said. "But I will."

"WHAT!?" Gabe cried. "Captain, you can't be serious!"

Before he could say anymore, Leon took the long winding coil of Lead standing by the side. He hooked it onto one of the wall's posts and swung downwards, gripping tightly onto the rope.

"CAPTAIN!" Gabe yelled from above.

Lower, Leon said as the rope slid down closer to the Mutant. Just let me get closer to him!

The Mutant Zombie looked up with its square face and giant, grotesque frown as Leon's rope swung closer to it and high up again. From where he was everything except the Mutant looked like pixels. He turned to Gabe and Richard and gave them a glance, letting them know exactly what they needed to do.

"FIRE YOUR ARROWS AT HIS FACE!" Gabe commanded the Archers.

The Bows were pulled back just as Leon reached the highest part of the rope's swing. His heart stopped for a moment. This is one chance, he said. Please let it be done right!

"FIRRREEEE!"

Multiple flaming Arrows shot into the Mutant's face.

RAAAAAAAAAAAAAAAAAAAAAAAAARRRRRRG GGGH!!!!!!!!!!!!!!!!!!

It's cry made the castle tremble. Leon's rope swung down as the Mutant clawed towards the Stone roof, once again exposing its neck. Leon gripped his Sword tightly and leapt from the rope downwards to the Mutant's neck. Jacob...Leon said in his mind. This is for you...

Leon screamed in rage as his Sword forced down and buried deep into the Mutant's neck.

AAAAAAAAAAAOOOOORORRRRAAAAAGGG GGGGGGHHHHH!!!!!!!!!!!!!!

Leon's knees feel onto the Mutant's cold and leathery skin, his Sword deeply embedded into it. He gripped it as the Mutant's hands raised into the air to swat him off. Leon gripped the Sword again and screamed as he dragged it across the Mutant's neck, drawing a deep wound into it until it screamed its final scream and slumped downwards.

The Mutant crashed onto the remaining mobs like a tumbling hill and Leon pulled out his weapon. The Mutant's back slid into a descent and before Leon knew it he was sliding towards the lava.

"CAPTAIN!" Richard called from above.

The rope swung towards Leon a second time and he grasped it, immediately being heaved up by his men and onto the roof. As he looked down, the lava poured onto the Mutant's head and set it on fire with the rest of the mobs. The lightning clashed one more time before it stopped along with the rain.

The dark sky turned into a pinkish twilight and the sun was rising. Slowly, the fire from the mobs disappeared and so did the Mutant. Leon's knees buckled with exhaustion and he fell to the floor, Gabe and Richard lifting him up while the other men surrounded him in concern.

"Captain!" Gabe said. "Captain, are you okay?"

Leon looked up to him with tired eyes and smiled.

"We did it…we did it…"

For the first time, Gabe's eyes began to water and he nodded.

"You're darn right we did."

Chapter 6: A Thorn in the Bush

Leon and the others rested for no more than thirty minutes before they set out onto the road again with the Horses. Nothing much had been left from the battle of the night, but the drawbridge was still damaged. They had built a Stone wall in its place. As they left, Leon looked up endearingly to the Stained Glass window of the Diamond Sword with the Emerald.

"I promise we'll come back to fix it," Leon said. "We'll do it in our gratitude and honor."

They set again, more than relieved to have Horses to do the work for them and by noon they had made more time than they could have imagined.

"Can you believe it?" Gabe had said. "We can make to the Emerald City in a day's time!"

"A day?" Leon asked in surprise. "After tonight?"

The soldiers were now sitting for a rest and eating a hearty meal after what seemed like forever. They did not however, let the Horses out of anyone's sight as they feared something could have happened again.

"No!" Gabe said. "Today!"

"Today!?" Leon exclaimed. "How can you possibly say that?"

Gabe bit into a Pork Chop and laid the Map out in front of him.

"I made a calculation using the block speed of the Horses and the comparison with the Map," he said. "These Horses are incredibly fast, if you haven't noticed. It wouldn't be surprising if they weren't enchanted."

Leon laughed.

"This is great then," Leon said. "We'll get the message there in no time. Lord Japheth will be pleased."

Gabe wrapped up the Map as Leon stood up and dusted his hands. He moved towards the soldiers to make the announcement.

"Alright, men!" he said. "According to Sir Gabe, we can make it to Emerald City within the day. I suggest we pack up now and be on our way so we don't have to stay in these blasted fields any longer."

The men cheered to that in merriment, glad to hear that soon they would be rid of Creeper Fields even for a while and they would be in the safety of the large and protected Emerald City. Quickly putting out the Furnace and saddling their Horses, the men began to ride through the fields again.

The sound of the Horses' hoofs were pleasing compared to walking through the Grass. The sun no longer felt that hot due to the speed and the wind that blew by them. For once, everything about the mission seemed to be assured to succeed. Leon rode up next to Richard who was practically racing with Horse.

"Slow down, Richard, you'll fall!" Leon said happily.

"Of course not!" Richard called from his Horse. "I was called the Wind Rider in my day! And I still got it now!"

Richard sped up in front of him until he was a silhouette in the bright sun. That old man is crazy, Leon said. I'm glad he's on my team. As he said so, Richard's Horse began to slow down and Leon was catching up.

"What?" Leon called out. "Is the Wind Rider losing speed already?"

But Richard wasn't replying or laughing. Instead, Richard was doubling over on his Horse, grunting and clutching his stomach. Leon's smile left his face as he grew closer to him and saw a painful grimace on the veteran.

"Richard?" Leon called.

Richard's body slid down the Saddle of his Horse and onto the Grass.

"Richard!" Leon cried.

He pulled on the reign of his Horse and got down to where the man was wincing in pain.

"Gaaaaah…." Richard muttered.

Leon rushed to his side and began shaking him.

"Richard, what's wrong!?" Leon said.

"I feel sick…" Richard mumbled. "My stomach…ugh…it's in pain!"

From behind him, Leon could hear the whinnies of other Horses and more groaning. His heart stopped as he saw his other men and Gabe also doubling over in pain. He turned to Richard for an answer.

"What's going on?" Leon said. "What's happening to all of you?"

Richard's eyes grew wide and he lifted a finger into the air.

"Cap—captain!"

Pain shot into Leon's shoulder blade as a sharp force pushed him to the side.

"Gaaaaaah!!!!!!!!!!" Leon shouted.

His hand went to the area with pain and he felt something long and wooden…an Arrow.

"What the heck is this!?" Leon said. "A Skeleton!?"

But as he turned, his shoulder throbbing and the pain making It hard to think, he saw something else. It was a soldier in loose Iron Armor with the Chain Mail dangling probably from being too big in size.

"Kai?" Leon said. "KAI!? YOU'RE THE TRAITOR!?"

The soldier walked up to him with the Bow equipped in his hands. A smile was on his face, but it wasn't one of sincerity.

"You stupid Captain," Kai said with a voice that no longer belonged to a boy. It was a harsh, cunning voice and Kai's bright eyes seemed to turn steely and sharp.

Leon tried to stand up, but Kai shot another arrow deep into Leon's knee.

"Aaaaaaaaaaaaaarrggggh!!!!" Leon yelled in pain.

He felt back to the ground on his right side, trying to move. Each turn he made felt like a knife of fire inside his affected joints and bones. He lifted his head and glared at Kai.

"How—how could you do this!?" Leon said. "How could you betray us, you're village men!?"

"My village men?" Kai sneered as he pulled back the Arrow in his Bow. "I think you're mistaken, my dear, dear Captain! I was never from the Diamond Village."

He pulled onto the loose Chest Plate of his armor to reveal a Gold shield imprinted on his Chain Mail.

"He's part of the Gold Legion!" Richard weakly exclaimed from where he was.

Kai laughed cruelly and walked up to Richard and Leon, but furiously staring up at him in disbelief.

"Bingo, old man!" Kai said. "I'm part of the Gold Legion, alright, and I've been their spy for this entire mission. I set up the TNT to let the Horses go. And those men who turned into Zombies in their rooms? I opened up a door and let them get bitten in their sleep as the Zombie began dying from burning. All of the men right now are suffering poisoning from the food I spiked. You would have, too, Captain Leon, had you not stupidly preferred Bread!"

Kai's thick Iron boot slammed down onto Leon's shoulder with the Arrow, adding to the burning pain.

"Aaaaaaaaaarrrgggggh!" Leon said.

"There's no use yelling," Kai said as he bent his head lower to Leon. "No one can hear you for miles and miles and miles. Now, I can put you out of your misery once you hand over the Letter."

Leon looked up to him as if he didn't understand.

"The what?" he said between clenched teeth.

"The Letter!" Kai said kicking Leon in the stomach. "The message for the Emerald City!"

Leon inhaled in pain and groaned. No, he thought. This can't be! We can't fail the mission! I can't give it!

"Give it now!" Kai shouted.

From Leon's peripheral vision, he could see Richard behind Kai. Slowly, Richard's trembling hands came to his pocket and pulled out a bright red Potion. Richard gave a glance to Leon. Distract him, his glance said. Leon immediately understood and he looked back up to Kai again.

"I don't have it!" Leon said.

"DON'T YOU LIE!" Kai roared, stomping his feet on the ground. "I KNOW YOU HAVE IT! I SAW YOU WITH THE ENVELOPE!"

Leon shook his head and let out a groan half in pretense.

"It's not with me," Leon said. "It's in...it's in my Horse's Saddle..."

"Your what!?" Kai said.

Leon lifted a finger towards his Horse that had now walked a bit of a distance from him.

"I slid it in the Saddle…" Leon said. "For safe…safe keeping…"

Half him was focusing on Kai who was now looking at the Horse greedily. Half of him was looking at Richard as he held a Splash Potion in his hand, ready to throw.

Kai glared down at Leon.

"If you're lying…" Kai said. "I'll shoot all your limbs and leave you the Zombies…"

Leon shook his head weakly.

"I'm…I'm not…! Please don't hurt me!"

Kai had to laugh at that.

"How pathetic!" Kai said. "All of that 'Don't give up!' nonsense of yours and I have you begging like a baby! You Diamond villagers are pathetic!"

Kai then rushed towards the Horse and began searching the Saddle, which the Horse didn't like at all. It whinnied and muttered.

"Stay still, you stupid animal!" Kai said.

"Now, Richard!" Leon said.

Richard threw the glass Splash Potion and red fluid splashed onto both of them.

"NO!" Kai shouted.

The pain immediately left Leon as the Potion of Healing absorbed into his armor and skin. He drew out his Sword and charged towards Kai, only to have his Diamond Sword met with Kai's enchanted Gold Sword.

"You traitor!" Leon shouted as he forced away Kai's Sword. Kai recovered from the push and swung back his weapon, laughing maniacally as he did.

"You're the one who recruited me!" Kai yelled. "You and your naiveté!"

Leon shouted again and forced Kai away. Kai swung his Sword, making Leon's tremble and push back.

"Don't bother fighting me!" Kai shouted. "My Gold Sword's enchantments make even your Diamond one as weak as a Wooden one!"

Leon swung again but was pushed back by the sheer force of Kai's Sword.

"Silly old Captain!" Kai said. "Can't even beat his own recruit in a Sword match!?"

Kai laughed hard and loud, his sound fueling Leon with white rage.

"Leon!" Richard called.

Leon turned around to see the old man back on his feet with a Diamond Sword glowing purple. He rushed towards Leon and threw it into the air.

"Use it!" he said. "It will match his weapon!"

The Sword somersaulted into the air. Leon grabbed it with his left hand and now held two Swords. Unexpectedly, Kai's triumphant expression shifted to surprise. He then sneered at Leon and glared at him.

"You still can't beat me!" Kai said. "I'm the most skilled swordsman in the entire Gold Nation!"

Kai moved forward as Leon put out both Swords into an X-shape. The Golden Sword's glow flickered and burned like hot fire against the cool shimmer of Leon's Diamond Sword. They pulled back and then engaged in heated battle as one swung after the other. Clashing, clashing, clashing, moving from the sides and charging. Stabbing, piercing, but both unable to touch one another…

It's an even match, Leon said worriedly. He's knees began to buckle and he realized that the Potion of Healing was wearing off due to the Arrow still causing damage in his shoulder and knee.

"You won't have much long now," Kai smiled as his Sword pressed against Leon's dual blades.

"I disagree!" Richard called.

As Kai and Leon turned to him, an Obsidian portal with a swirling purple vortex stood beside him. Richard lifted his hands in the air.

"O Nether that doth punish the most wretched!" he called. "Take with thee a soul to engulf in your inferno! A traitor and killer and selfish man! Take he, which is Kai, with you NOW!"

The purple vortex flickered and then from a flat plane turned into a swirling whirlpool. The wind stirred, vacuuming into the purplish chaos that was the Nether, but Leon's feet seemed stuck to the ground. The Golden Sword lifted away from Leon's weapons and Kai's eyes bulged widely as two glowing blue eyes looked at him from the vortex.

"No," Kai said. "NO! NO! I DON'T WANT TO GO!"

There was a laugh in the air and it seemed to be one belonging to a girl. A husky, sweet voice, but also one filled with insanity. Kai's feet lifted from the ground as from the vortex came a large, but beautifully clawed cream hand, embracing Kai in its devious clutches.

"NO!" Kai screamed in terror. "I DON'T WANT TO GO! YOU CAN'T MAKE ME! YOU CAN'T MAKE MEEEEEEEEEEEEEEE!!!!!!!!!!!!!!!!"

The hand pulled him in and with a flash, lightning came from the clear sky and destroyed the Obsidian portal into bits and pieces. The stirred wind turned into a quiet breeze and Kai's screams were no longer heard.

Richard stooped down to his knees and wiped his brow.

"Hoo!" he said. "That was close, eh, Captain?"

Leon walked up to him, still stupefied and shocked, looking at Richard in questioning.

"What...what was that?" Leon asked.

Richard gave a crooked smile.

"I built a Nether Portal while you fought," Richard said. "I had a feeling the fight wouldn't hold out long. I also used a spell I learned from Priest Shep. He says it was used before against Witches. I thought why not use it now?"

For a while, Leon just stood there and looked at Richard and then he did the oddest thing: he hugged him. Leon's arms wrapped tightly around the old man like he was his own father. Leon then realized his eyes were wet with tears.

"Thank you!" Leon said. "Thank you so much! We can finish the mission now! We really can!"

Richard gave out a small laugh.

"Yes, indeed," he said. "We should get on our way. But let's heal our friends of Food Poisoning, shall we?"

It was the happiest Leon had felt in so long and aside from getting the message to the Emerald City he had one wish left. If only you could see me, Jacob, he thought. If only you could see me pass through Creeper Fields. I promise, one day, we'll do it together. You and I.

Prologue: The Message

In the Emerald Palace, King Ozac was sitting anxiously in his Emerald-encrusted throne. His gray hair was pulled back by a green circlet and he watched the Emerald-colored halls as the large metal doors opened to reveal a group of men wearing the Diamond Emblem on their armor.

A man near the Door blew his trumpet in fanfare.

"Your Highness," he said. "May I present the messengers from the Diamond Village with urgent news from Lord Japheth."

King Ozac lifted out a hand.

"I welcome you, brothers from the Diamond Village," he said. "I bid you come closer."

The men, sooty and worn out, sweaty and exhausted, marched prouder than the richest, finest men in the world. The citizens watched as they slowly made their procession towards the King, the leader wearing a blue cape holding an envelope sealed with wax.

The men knelt down in front of the King.

"Your Majesty," the one in the blue cape said. "I am Leon, Captain of the Diamond Village's Guards. My men and I come with a message from our Lord Japheth. Please allow me to read it to you."

"I allow you to do so," King Ozac said.

Leon rose from his place and used a letter opener to cut the envelope open. His eyes scanned the Letter silently as King Ozac's heart throbbed in nervousness to hear the news. Finally, Leon's blue eyes met with the King's and he uttered the words that would change the history of the era.

"It is time."

THE END.

Made in the USA
San Bernardino, CA
19 December 2014